HURRY UP!

A Book About Slowing Down

written by
Kate Dopirak

illustrated by
Christopher Silas Neal

Beach Lane Books • New York London Toronto Sydney New Delhi

Hurry up!

Hurry down.

Hurry round and round . . .

and round.

Hurry here.

Hurry there.

Hurry, scurry everywhere!

Hurry out.

Hurry in.

Hurry if you want to win.

Hurry so you'll reach the **top.**

Hurry

Hurry

Hurry

Slow things down.

Take a break.

Look around, for goodness' sake.

Breathe it in.

Blow it out.

This is what it's all about.

Make a wish.

Take a walk.

Listen to the forest talk.

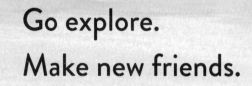

Go explore.

Make new friends.

Find out where the rainbow ends.

Count the stars,
easy does.

Marvel at the nighttime buzz.

Mosey home.

Stretch and yawn.

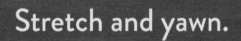

Race is off,
and rest is on.

No more fast—
slooooooow instead.

Dreams and lazy days ahead.

For Joey and Bobby, my inspiration—K. D.

For Jasper and River:
don't forget to slow down every now and then—C. S. N.

BEACH LANE BOOKS

An imprint of Simon & Schuster Children's Publishing Division

1230 Avenue of the Americas, New York, New York 10020

Text copyright © 2020 by Kate Dopirak

Illustrations copyright © 2020 by Christopher Silas Neal

All rights reserved, including the right of reproduction in whole or in part in any form.

BEACH LANE BOOKS is a trademark of Simon & Schuster, Inc.

For information about special discounts for bulk purchases, please contact

Simon & Schuster Special Sales at 1-866-506-1949 or business@simonandschuster.com.

The Simon & Schuster Speakers Bureau can bring authors to your live event.

For more information or to book an event, contact the Simon & Schuster Speakers Bureau

at 1-866-248-3049 or visit our website at www.simonspeakers.com.

Book design by Lauren Rille

The text for this book was set in Brandon Grotesque.

The illustrations for this book were rendered in mixed media.

Manufactured in China

0220 SCP

First Edition

10 9 8 7 6 5 4 3 2 1

CIP data for this book is available from the Library of Congress.

ISBN 978-1-5344-2497-5

ISBN 978-1-5344-2498-2 (eBook)